FLYER books are for confident readers who can take on the challenge of a longer

Táin Bó Cuailgne (The Ca... main story in the *Red Branch* cycle of stories which has come down to us out of the Celtic past. The text is drawn from manuscripts of the twelfth and later centuries, and from oral tradition. It is a robust saga of heroes, sinister magic, warriors grappling in single combat, and battles fought during an invasion of Ulster by the army of Queen Maeve of Connacht. All that stands between Ulster and defeat is the boy hero, Cúchulainn, sometimes referred to as the Irish Achilles. The war was sparked off by an attempt to carry out a cattle raid in Cooley, County Louth. This telling is geared to the interest level and reading competence of the young reader, in the hope that it will provide them with a fascinating tale in its own right, and also serve to introduce them to the finest jewel in early Irish literature.

Can YOU spot the aeroplane hidden in the story?

FRANK MURPHY

Having worked as a school principal, and written poetry, school books and short stories in his spare time, Frank wrote his first novel for children, *Lockie and Dadge*, when he retired. It went on to win a Bisto Book of the Year merit award and the Eilís Dillon Memorial Award.

KIERON BLACK

Irish cartoonist Kieron Black graduated in graphic information design five years ago, but still isn't exactly sure why. Living next to the beach in Strangford, County Down, he is helped in his cartoon and illustration work by an indeterminate number of frogs, eight chickens, three cats and Bosun, his large, enthusiastic but generally skill-free dalmation.

PRONUNCIATION GUIDE	
Ailill	al-il
Ath Gabhla	awth gav-la
Cruachan	croo-a-*ch*un
Cúchulainn	cu-*ch*ul-in
Dáire	daw-i-re
Emain Macha	ev-in ma-*ch*a
Ferdia	fer-dee-uh
Fraech	fray*ch*
Laeg	lay*gh*
Loch	lu*ch* (*u* as in c*u*t)
MacRoth	mok-roth
Morrígan	morr-ee-*gh*un

Note: *ch* and *gh* are guttural

The Big Fight

THE STORY OF THE TÁIN

Frank Murphy

Illustrated by Kieron Black

THE O'BRIEN PRESS
DUBLIN

First published 1999 by The O'Brien Press Ltd,
20 Victoria Road, Dublin 6, Ireland.
Tel: +353 1 4923333; Fax: +353 1 4922777
E-mail: books@obrien.ie
Website: www.obrien.ie
Reprinted 2000, 2003.

ISBN: 0-86278-451-4

British Library Cataloguing-in-Publication Data
Murphy, Frank, 1949-
The big fight : the story of the Tain. - (O'Brien flyers ; 3)
1.Children's stories
I.Title
823.9'14[J]

3   4   5   6   7   8   9   10
03   04   05   06   07   08

Typesetting, editing, layout, design: The O'Brien Press Ltd
Cover and internal illustrations: Kieron Black
Printing: Cox & Wyman Ltd

CHAPTER 1

The Brown Bull

Long, long ago Maeve was the warrior queen of Connacht. She was married to a prince called Ailill. They lived in a fine palace in Cruachan, and they were both very rich.

One night Maeve and Ailill were talking about how rich they were.

'You are a lucky queen,' said Ailill. 'You are married to **the** richest person in Ireland.'

'**Oh No,**' said Maeve. '**I** am the richest. Not you!'

'But I have more than you,' Ailill
boasted.

'All right, then,' said Maeve, 'let us
count all we have!'

Next day they counted all they
had: all the jewels, the gold, the silver,
the cattle, the horses,
the gardens,
the palaces.

Maeve had just as much as Ailill –
except for **one** thing ...

Ailill had a **huge** bull with white horns, and Maeve had nothing to match that.

Maeve was **very** angry because
Ailill had more than she had.

'Send for MacRoth!' she yelled.
MacRoth was her **wise man**.

'Where can I find a better bull than
Ailill's?' she asked MacRoth.

'In Cooley, in Ulster, there is a man called Dáire,' MacRoth told Maeve.

'And Dáire has a big brown bull. It is the **only** bull in Ireland that is better than Ailill's bull.'

'Go to Dáire and tell him to lend that bull to me,' Maeve ordered.

Next day MacRoth and nine
warriors marched to Dáire's farm
in Cooley.

Dáire said, **Yes**, he would lend his
Great Brown Bull to Maeve.

MacRoth and his warriors sat down
to rest in Dáire's house after supper.
They talked of many things.

'Lucky for Dáire he gave the bull,' a warrior said. 'If he had refused, we would have taken it by force.'

One of Dáire's servants was listening to the warriors' talk. He went at once and told his master what was said.

Dáire shouted in a **rage**. 'Tell MacRoth I've changed my mind. They cannot have the bull. And they must leave – at once.'

When Maeve was told that Dáire would not lend the bull to her, she said, 'Very well, we will march into Ulster and take it from him.'

CHAPTER 2

Maeve's Army on the March

Maeve and Ailill gathered a **great** army at their palace in Cruachan.

Warriors from every part of Ireland came to join the army.

Fergus was one of
the leaders of Maeve's
army. He was a
great warrior
and a very
wise man.

But he didn't want to fight against
Ulster because Ulster had a brave
young warrior called **Cúchulainn**,
and Fergus and Cúchulainn were
friends.

At that time the fighting men of Ulster were lying on their backs and could not get up. They had been put under a **magic** spell.

They were as weak as babies and could not fight.

But the women and children of
Ulster had not fallen under the spell.
And the young warrior Cúchulainn
was spared as well. If Ulster needed
him, he could fight.

In the early days of winter the Connacht army marched into Ulster. They were on their way to Cooley. They went over hills, across deep rivers, and through dark woods. Their march was easy because the men of Ulster were nowhere to be seen.

Cúchulainn went out to stop the Connacht men at the river crossing at **Ath Gabhla**.

With only **one** blow of his sword, he cut down a tree-fork and stuck it in the middle of the river so that no chariot could pass by on either side.

The Connacht army came to
the river crossing, and they saw
the tree-fork. A message was
written on it:

THIS TREE FORK HAS
BEEN CUT DOWN AND
THROWN HERE BY ONE
MAN. THE CONNACHT
ARMY MAY NOT PASS
THIS PLACE UNTIL ONE
OF ITS SOLDIERS,
BUT NOT FERGUS,
DOES THE SAME

Cúchulainn did this,' Fergus said to Maeve. 'He is only seventeen years old, but he is the son of a **god** and skilled in war and the **magic** arts.'

Many of the soldiers tried to pull the tree-fork from the river, but they could not move it.

In the end Fergus had to take the tree-fork from the water.

The soldiers could see that it had been cut down by just **one** blow, and they were afraid.

CHAPTER 3

The Morrígan

The Connacht army marched on until they came to another river.

But the **super warrior**, Cúchulainn, had been there before them once again.

He knocked a huge oak tree into the river and wrote a message on its bark:

Thirty warriors tried and failed.
Every one of them came crashing
down on the tree.

Maeve sent her great warrior, **Fraech,** to fight Cúchulainn at the river. They fought in the water, twisting and turning, falling and rising again.

But Fraech went under the water and was drowned.
His companions carried his body back to camp, and Maeve and her soldiers were very **sad**.

Then Fergus leapt his chariot across the fallen tree, and the army moved on.

Day after day warriors were sent to fight Cúchulainn, but he killed them **all**.

Maeve then thought of a way to trick Cúchulainn. She divided the army into **two** groups.

One group moved out from the camp and Cúchulainn followed them. Then Maeve led the other group to Cooley.

THAT WAY!

Some of Maeve's men found the **Great Brown Bull**. They drove Dáire and his guards away and they captured the bull.

But the bull broke free, and went on a crazy run through the camp. It killed fifty soldiers in that mad rush.

31

When Cúchulainn found out that he had been tricked, he went to a hill above the Connacht camp. He pelted the soldiers with stones.

Maeve was very angry, so she sent for the **Morrígan**, and asked her to help.

The Morrígan was a **goddess of war**. People were afraid of her because she had evil powers. She could change her shape to become anything she wished to be.

Morrígan changed herself into a
beautiful woman, and she asked
Cúchulainn to give up the fighting for
her sake.

Cúchulainn said '**No!**' and she was
mad with rage.

'I will be your enemy from now on,' Morrígan said. 'One day you will be in a battle, and I will come in the shape of an **eel**. And I will help to kill you.'

Maeve sent many warriors against Cúchulainn, but he killed them all.

Then she sent out a warrior named **Loch**, and he was brave and strong. Loch and Cúchulainn fought like tigers in the river.

From nowhere an **eel** came swimming up the river. It wrapped itself around Cúchulainn's legs and he fell down into the water.

Loch rushed in and struck the fallen warrior with his sword.

Cúchulainn was badly wounded.
He lay on his back in the water.

But he had a **magic spear** called
the **Ga Bolga**. He threw the spear
with his foot and it struck Loch and
killed him on the spot.

Then Cúchulainn chased the eel, but it changed into a **wolf**.

He chased the wolf, but it changed into a **heifer**.

He chased the heifer, but he didn't catch it. The heifer ran away.

CHAPTER 4

The Boy Soldiers

In the evening Cúchulainn sat by the campfire with **Laeg**, his chariot driver. They could see the Connacht army, and their weapons were shining as the sun went down.

Cúchulainn flew into a **rage** again when he saw how many soldiers were against him.

He shouted out his warrior's cry. The cry was so loud that the spirits of the air joined in.

The enemy army trembled when they heard Cúchulainn's battle cry. One hundred warriors were so **afraid** that they fell down and died.

Cúchulainn was weak from all his wounds. **Lugh**, his father in the spirit world, came to help him, and he put the tired warrior into a deep sleep. While Cúchulainn was asleep, Lugh cleaned his wounds and put healing herbs on them.

Cúchulainn did not wake for three whole days and three whole nights.

While Cúchulainn was asleep, the boy soldiers came from the royal palace of Ulster, at **Emain Macha**. They came to help him in the fight.

Maeve gave orders to her army. 'Attack those Ulster soldiers. They are only boys!'

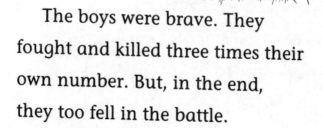

The boys were brave. They fought and killed three times their own number. But, in the end, they too fell in the battle.

When Cúchulainn woke, he was strong and ready for battle again. He swore he would get **revenge** for the boy soldiers.

He put on his battle dress and took up his weapons.

His chariot driver, Laeg, got
the chariot ready.

The madness of war came on Cúchulainn, and his face and body twisted and swelled. He looked like some awful **monster**.

Cúchulainn got into the chariot and raced into the enemy camp. The Connacht soldiers ran out of their tents and rushed right and left.

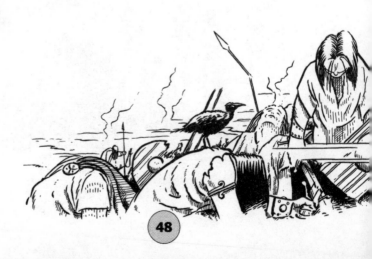

But there was **no escape** for many of the men.

When Cúchulainn had gone, Maeve came out of her hiding place. She saw the ground covered with the bodies of her fighting men.

CHAPTER 5

Cúchulainn, Ferdia and Fergus

Then Maeve sent for **Ferdia**, her greatest warrior, and she asked him to fight Cúchulainn.

Ferdia and Cúchulainn were best friends, so Ferdia did not want to fight, but Maeve made him do it.

On the first day of their battle they fought with shield and spear. Nobody won that day. In the evening they helped to heal each other's wounds, and they shared their food.

On the second day it was the same.

On the third day they fought so hard that, by the end, they were very weak. That night they stayed apart.

On the fourth day they fought in the river. As the day went on Ferdia was winning.

But Cúchulainn called for the **Ga Bolga,** his magic spear. He threw it with his foot, so fast and fierce that it passed through shield and armour and struck Ferdia's body. Ferdia fell into the stream and he lay there, dying.

Cúchulainn was sad. He lifted his old friend in his arms and brought him to the river bank. Cúchulainn was so weak that he fell down in a faint beside the dying Ferdia.

Afterwards Laeg, the chariot driver, took Cúchulainn to a safe place and healed his wounds.

And then the spell was lifted from the men of Ulster. They recovered from their weakness.

Conor, the king of Ulster, led out his warriors to face the Connacht army.

The two armies met at evening time, but Conor and Ailill agreed not to fight until the sun came up.

That night the **Morrígan** cried out in the dark. She cried because of all the men who would lose their lives in the battle.

The armies heard her, and a hundred men fell down and died in fright, even before the battle began.

All through the next day they fought. As the evening came, the Ulstermen were driven back across the river.

But then the battle madness came again upon Cúchulainn, and he rushed into the fight. He swung his sword from side to side, and cleared a path through the Connacht army. Then he came face to face with **Fergus**.

Fergus had promised Cúchulainn that, if they ever met in battle, Fergus would give **way** to his old friend.

Fergus would not break a promise, so he left the field of battle with his fighting men.

Maeve and her warriors saw
what happened, and they ran
away. But on their way they
came upon the Great Brown Bull.
They captured it and brought it
back to the palace at **Cruachan**.

CHAPTER 6

The Battle of the Bulls

It was the day after the battle. The Connacht warriors who had escaped were watching the **Great Brown Bull of Cooley** facing the **White-Horned Bull of Ailill** on the lawn at Cruachan.

The bulls charged and their great battle began.

The bulls fought through all that day and into the night that followed.

Darkness came down, and the men could not see the battle. But they could hear the bulls roaring, and the clash of their horns, and the drumming of their hooves.

When the next day dawned, the men saw the **Great Brown Bull** limping towards them from the east, and pieces of the White-Horned Bull were hanging like rags from his horns.

The battle of the bulls was over. The Great Brown Bull went back towards Cooley, but he didn't get home. He died on the way at a place which is called, to this very day, **The Ridge of the Bull.**

Ailill and Maeve made **peace** with Conor. They returned to Cruachan and the Ulstermen marched proudly home to Emain Macha.